ARNOLD LOBEL

COLOR BY

ADRIANNE LOBEL

THE FROGS AND TOADS ALL SANG

HARPERCOLLINS*PUBLISHERS*

In memory of Crosby and George Bonsall

—Arnold Lobel

For Papa

—Adrianne Lobel

The Frogs and Toads All Sang

Copyright © 2009 by the Estate of Arnold Lobel

Manufactured in China

For information address HarperCollins Children's Books, a division of HarperCollins Publishers,

195 Broadway, New York, NY 10007.

www.harpercollinschildrens.com

Library of Congress Cataloging-in-Publication Data

Lobel, Arnold.

The frogs and toads all sang / Arnold Lobel ; color by Adrianne Lobel. — 1st ed.

v. cm.

Summary: Presents a linked collection of ten short stories in rhyme featuring frogs, toads, and polliwogs.

Contents: The frogs and toads all sang — Miss Frog went in the kitchen — I love to eat — Polliwog school — Bright green frog — Made for toads — There was a frog — Night — A toad was feeling . . . — One summer night.

ISBN 978-0-06-180022-1 (trade bdg.) — ISBN 978-0-06-180023-8 (lib. bdg.)

[1. Stories in rhyme. 2. Frogs—Fiction. 3. Toads—Fiction. 4. Tadpoles—Fiction.] I. Lobel, Adrianne, ill. II. Title.

PZ8.3.L82Fro 2009   2008051768

[E]—dc22   CIP

                                                                                                                        AC

Typography by Martha Rago

17 18   SCP   10 9 8 7 6 5 4   ❖ First Edition

CONTENTS

INTRODUCTION

Justin Schiller, a collector and an expert in the field of children's book art, is a portly gentleman who looks like a character that might have been drawn by my papa, Arnold Lobel. In September 2008, Justin called me about an estate auction of Crosby Bonsall, where he purchased some Lobel books that had been handmade and given as gifts.

Half a generation older than my young bohemian parents, Crosby and George Bonsall were a sophisticated and well-traveled couple. Though they seemed fancy to us, I remember them as wonderfully fun, warm, and magical people who always knew how to entertain my little brother and me. Crosby Bonsall was an established author and illustrator of children's books. In fact, her best-known book, *Who's a Pest?*, is still in print.

It is amazing to me, as a grown-up with a small child of my own, that Papa ever found time to write and draw every day, clean the house (he liked to vacuum), do the dishes, and put us to bed—and *then* write and illustrate more books as gifts for friends. When I saw how complete these "gifts" were, I thought that they might be of interest to a publisher. I contacted the esteemed editor Susan Hirschman, a great old friend who discovered Papa and was his first editor. She put me in touch with Susan Katz, president and publisher of HarperCollins Children's Books, who immediately recognized their value, and this new book was quickly under way.

I think that the poems and pictures are important in the grand arc of Arnold Lobel's work. This was the first time he wrote about frogs and toads. Also, the exuberant vitality of the sketches is not representative of the kind of work he was doing for publication at the time. The sixties was the decade of Mister Muster, *Small Pig*, and *Giant John*, among others; his work was delightful but much tighter and more cartoonish, very much influenced by the popular norm. These private sketches, not meant for anyone's eyes but those of friends, have a confidence and a liveliness that anticipates his mature work in books such as the Frog and Toad series, *Fables*, and *The Arnold Lobel Book of Mother Goose*.

It was into these later works that I delved to find a watercolor technique befitting Papa's pencil sketches. There is no better way to fully understand and appreciate an artist than by trying to copy him. As a stage designer by profession, I have no fear of designing huge shows for theaters that seat hundreds, sometimes thousands of people. This would have terrified Papa the same way I am terrified by the thought of anything I do actually being *published*. To shake myself of fear and to produce watercolors with the same freedom and effortlessness that approached Papa's, I gave myself a long warming-up period.

HarperCollins provided a stack of the original line illustrations printed on watercolor paper. I colored each illustration over many times. I used Papa's preferred Dr. Martin's dyes, worked very wet, and with a big brush. I kept in mind one of the things Papa taught me as a very young artist: *Don't be afraid to color outside of the lines!*

I hope that in small measure I have done well by him. Working on this book has been very enjoyable. Not only have I come to appreciate more deeply how good he was at what he did, but I discovered something even more important. Whenever the family went on vacation, all Papa wanted was to go home and get back to his drawing table. Now I understand that, for Arnold Lobel, there was no better fun to be had.

—*Adrianne Lobel*

The Frogs and Toads All Sang

"We're going to have a party,"
The frogs and toads all sang.
"We've got lemonade with ice cubes
And paper lamps to hang."
The ladies wore long dresses,
And the gentlemen wore pants.
The orchestra was ready,
So they all began to dance.
They danced in the meadow.
They danced in the street.
They danced in the lemonade
Just to cool their feet.

Miss Frog Went in the Kitchen

Miss Frog went in the kitchen
To bake some apple pies.
The little frogs were watching
With hunger in their eyes.
Miss Frog went in the kitchen
To make a sugar bun.
The little frogs were waiting
Until the bun was done.
But when the stuff was finished
And cooling on the shelf . . .
Miss Frog cried, "Go away, you fools!"
And ate them all herself.

I Love to Eat

"I love to eat,"
A fat toad cried.
"I eat all day,"
He cried with pride.
"I eat and eat
Until it hurts,
Then finish up
With three desserts.
And when the
Evening darkness comes,
I light the lamp
And eat the crumbs."

Polliwog School

Underneath

The lily pads,

Where the mud is cool,

Many little polliwogs

Swim their way to school.

"We go to class each day,"

Said one.

"And all we do is wiggle.

We do not read . . .

We do not write . . .

We only squirm and giggle."

BRIGHT GREEN FROG

A bright green frog
With slippery skin
Played waltzes
On a violin.
But while he played
With skill and grace,
He wore a frown
Upon his face.
"I fiddle well."
He sighed.
"And yet . . .
I'd rather play
The clarinet."

Made for Toads

A sunny day
Is made for toads
To play and leap
Down dusty roads.

A rainy day is made for frogs

To swim in swamps

And under logs.

In weather gray

Or weather bright,

For some, the day

Will be just right.

THERE WAS A FROG

There was a frog
Who had a car.
He drove it fast.
He drove it far.
He traveled
Fifty days and nights
And never
Looked at traffic lights.
"I learned to drive
Quite easily,
But I never learned
To stop," said he.

NIGHT

Two toads sat
Dozing on a rock.
Said one, "I think
We need a clock."
The other said,
"I do agree.
A clock for you
And one for me.
Then when we wake
And there's no light . . .
We'll always know
That it is night."

A Toad Was Feeling . . .

A toad was feeling
Sad and grumpy
Because his skin
Was rough and lumpy.
"My skin is bad,"
Said he. "I'll hide it."
He bought a coat
And jumped inside it.
"And now," he said,
"I do not worry. . . .
Outside I'm nicely
Soft and furry."

One Summer Night

One summer night
In early June,
A frog looked upward
At the moon.
He said, "I'll jump
Right on that thing
Without the use
Of jet or spring."
He counted three,
Then jumped quite high
And hit the moon
In late July.